www.enchantedlionbooks.com

Text copyright © 2015 by Michaël Escoffier
Illustrations copyright © 2015 by Kris Di Giacomo

First edition published by Enchanted Lion Books,
351 Van Brunt Street, Brooklyn, NY 11231

ISBN 978-1-59270-189-6

First edition 2015
Design and layout: Kris Di Giacomo
Printed in China by South China Printing Co.

10 9 8 7 6 5 4 3 2 1

# WHERE'S THE BABOON?

written by Michaël Escoffier

illustrated by Kris Di Giacomo

ENCHANTED LION BOOKS
NEW YORK

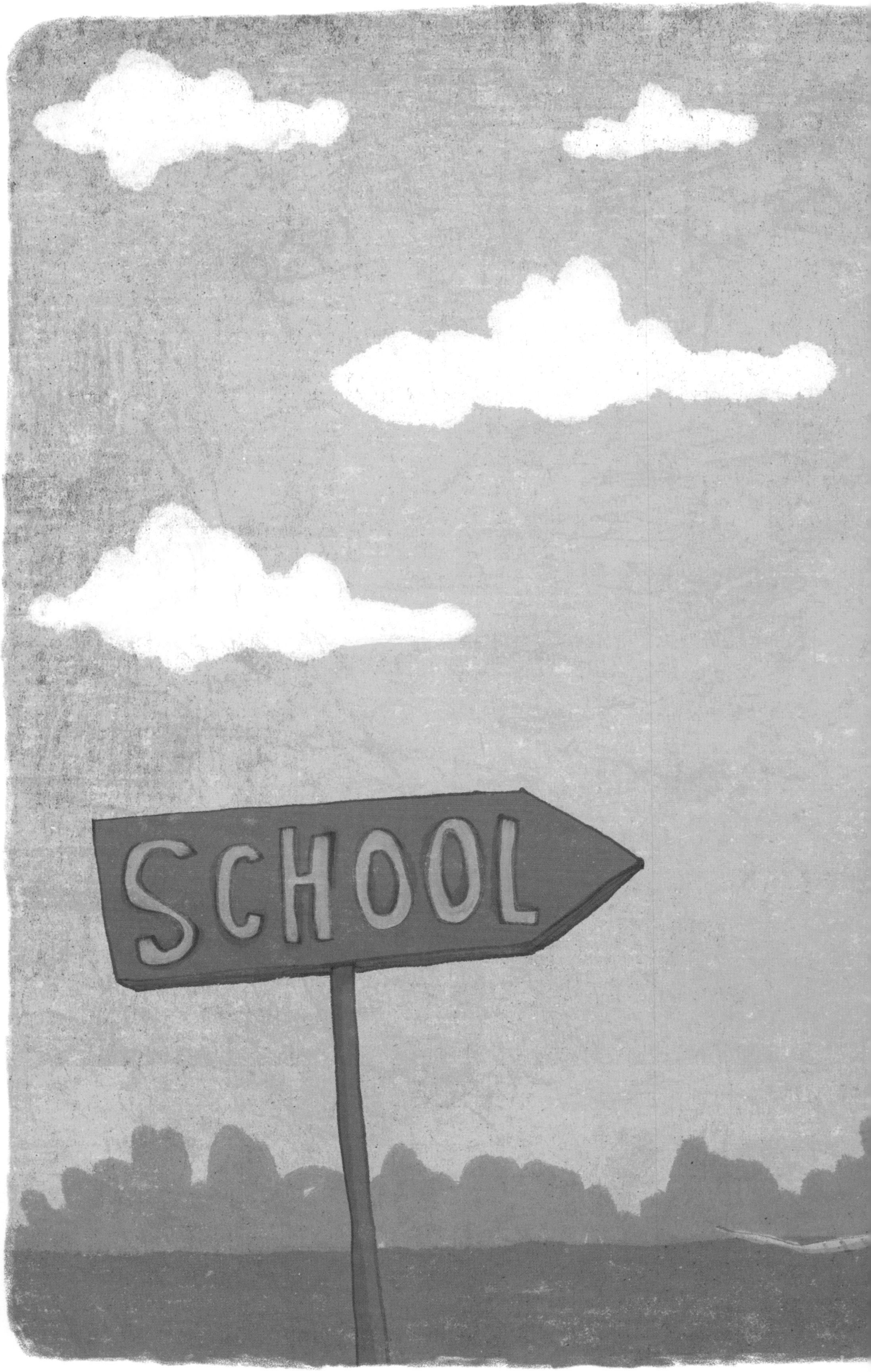
SCHOOL

# Who is the headmaster?

Who brought an **apple**?

Who is hiding behind
the castle?

# Who made this painting?

# Who is copying the rabbit?

# Who is the **clown**?

# Who is making
# snowflakes?

Who is making
mischief?

# Who is playing with the **seagull**?

Who left these
droppings?

# Who is having a
## birthday?

# Wait!
# Who is missing?

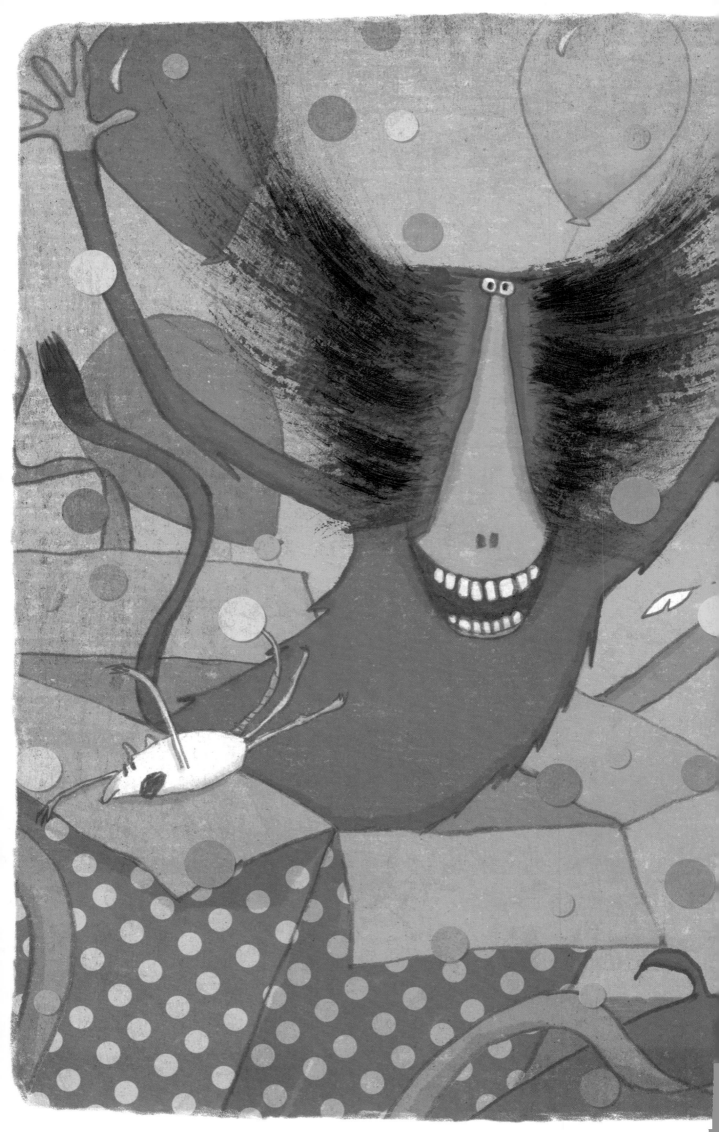

pig

rat

mice

toad

hamster cow